CALL ME LITTLE ECHO HAWK

THE STORY OF A NAME

by

TERRY
ECHOHAWK

illustrated by

JIM
MADSEN

ISBN: 1-55517-804-9
v.1

Published by CFI,
an imprint of Cedar Fort, Inc.
925 N. Main, Springville, Utah, 84663
www.cedarfort.com

Distributed by:

Jacket illustration by Jim Madsen
Jacket and book design by Nicole Williams
Cover design © 2005 by Lyle Mortimer

Printed in Hong Kong
10 9 8 7 6 5 4 3 2 1

Savannah EchoHawk peeked into the kitchen, where her grandfather sat alone at the table in the early morning sunlight. The house was very quiet, and no one else in her family was awake. This was the first time her grandfather had come for a visit, and it was the first time Savannah had ever seen him.

He had thick black hair streaked with grey, wrinkles around his dark eyes, and small round glasses that sat on his nose. She tried to tiptoe back to her room before he saw her, but she stopped in her tracks when she heard his deep voice.

"Don't go, Little Echo Hawk."

Savannah turned and saw her grandfather smiling and motioning for her to come into the kitchen.

"Why did you call me that?" she asked, moving closer.

Grandfather took off his glasses and laid them on the table. "When you came sneaking down the hallway, you reminded me of a little boy who wore moccasins just like the ones you have on."

"Who was he?" asked Savannah, as she edged closer to her grandfather.

"His name was Echo Hawk. He lived a long time ago. I'm guessing you don't know about him."

Savannah shook her head.

"I think it's time you heard about this little boy—and about how you got your last name."

"I would like to know about Echo Hawk and my name," she said. "Tell me."

Grandfather picked up Savannah and placed her on his knee. "Your name is very special. It is important to know where your name comes from. Stories about the people who had your name before you might help you to know which paths to follow and how best to walk in your own moccasins.

"The little boy was an Indian—a Native American like you and me. He was my great-grandfather and lived not so very long ago."

"He wore moccasins like me?" Savannah asked.

"Yes," her grandfather answered. "His moccasins were made of buffalo or deer skin. They were the only shoes he had, and he wore them every day. His hair was black as the night, his skin was golden brown, and his eyes were dark like the night sky. He was from the Pawnee tribe."

Grandfather paused for a moment, his eyes taking on a faraway look.

"Echo Hawk lived in the lands of the Pawnee Indians. Today, if you traveled to the places where he ran and played, you would be in the state of Nebraska. The lands where he grew up were filled with many trees, wild fruits and nuts, deer and bison, wild turkeys, and fish in the streams and rivers.

"When Echo Hawk was a child, he lived with his family in a lodge made from dirt and grass. His family grew corn and vegetables near their lodge. His father used a bow and arrow and rode a horse to hunt buffalo. If Echo Hawk, his family, and other members of his tribe followed the buffalo herds in the summer, they would live in tepees made from animal skins."

"Like camping?" Savannah asked.

"Yes," said Grandfather, "just like camping."

"As Echo Hawk became a young man, he grew to be six feet tall. Some say that he rode a black horse and was a brave warrior for his tribe. He used a bow and arrow with skill. People said he could shoot three arrows quickly while riding his horse by holding one arrow in his mouth, one in his bow hand, and one nocked against his bowstring, ready to shoot. He could also shoot a gun so well that he never returned from a hunt without food for his family.

"The tribal elders who tell stories of him say he was a kind and giving man. He raised horses and often gave them to members of his own tribe and other tribes too. He would also give food to tribal families that didn't have enough."

Grandfather continued, "When Echo Hawk was born, his father named him Big Crow, but when he became a young man he received a new name from his tribe."

"Will I get a new name?" asked Savannah.

"You won't get a new name, Savannah, but you might get a nickname—a name your parents or brothers or sisters give you, a name that describes you," Grandfather explained.

"Pawnee Indians usually got their names from older members of their tribe who watched them and saw the things they did. To the Pawnee, a hawk is a very good hunter. It is also one of few birds that do not sing.

"The Pawnee elders watched Big Crow and named him for the hawk, who is a strong warrior but who never sings or talks of his own deeds. The other members of the tribe, however, did talk about the good things Big Crow did, echoing them throughout the village. He became known as the hawk whose deeds are echoed, or Echo Hawk. In the Pawnee language, they called him *Kutawakutsu Tuwaku-ah*."

Savannah couldn't say the Pawnee name, so her grandfather pronounced it slowly for her: "Ku-ta-wa-kut-su Tu-wah-ku-ah."

Grandfather continued, "The Pawnees made drawings on their horses, the walls of their lodges and tepees, and their clothes to show who they were. Echo Hawk's family used drawings of the hawk to show which family they belonged to."

"Please show me what the hawk looks like," said Savannah.

Grandfather reached for a pencil and drew the Echo Hawk bird. Savannah traced the lines of the hawk with her finger and then looked up at her grandfather with a smile.

He smiled in return and said, "When I saw you running in your moccasins, it made my heart happy. It is important that you learn of Echo Hawk and always remember him and the Pawnee people who are a part of you."

"I will always remember," Savannah answered. "I promise."

Grandfather looked deeply into Savannah's big brown eyes and said, "Savannah, I hope this story will help you remember to be proud that you are a Native American, to help others whenever you can, and to have courage to do what is right. Make Echo Hawk proud that you carry his name."

"I am proud," Savannah said, hugging her grandfather. "Proud to be Little Echo Hawk!"

THE STORY OF MY NAME

My full name is _____

My first name is _____

I was given this name because

_____

_____

_____

My middle name (or nickname) is _____

I was given this name because

_____

_____

_____

My last name is _____

This name comes from

_____

_____

_____

Things I want to always remember about why my name is special

_____

_____

_____

_____

_____

FAMILY TREE
(PEDIGREE CHART)

_____
ME

_____
MY FATHER

_____
MY MOTHER

_____
GRANDFATHER

_____
GRANDMOTHER

_____
GRANDFATHER

_____
GRANDMOTHER

GREAT-GRANDPARENTS

_____

_____

_____

_____

_____

_____

_____

_____

AUTHOR'S NOTE

I have heard the oral history of Echo Hawk repeated by members of my husband's family for many years. It is a story rich in culture, tradition, and pride.

Echo Hawk was born around 1855. Though he passed away more than a century ago, his posterity is proud to be Native American. Echo Hawk was encouraged by the federal government to take the name "Price" as his surname because it was more familiar and accepted by society. He refused, insisting on keeping Echo Hawk as his family's surname. Today, direct descendants have chosen to spell their names as Echo Hawk, EchoHawk, Echohawk, or Echo-hawk, and can be found mostly in Oklahoma, Colorado, Utah, and Idaho.

Several characteristics define the Echo Hawk family. They are proud to be enrolled as members of the federally recognized Pawnee tribe. They are also proud to be American citizens who have fought to defend the freedoms and liberty of this great land that has given them both pain and promise. Many members of Echo Hawk's family served their country in the armed forces in World War II, Korea, Vietnam, and Desert Storm. Many still serve today. These respected individuals are highly honored among members of their tribe.

Echo Hawk's descendants have also served in public office. Larry EchoHawk, a great-grandson who is the husband of the author of this book, became the first Native American to be elected as a state attorney general, serving in Idaho from 1990 to 1994. Currently he teaches law at the J. Reuben Clark Law School at Brigham Young University.

Many Echo Hawk family members carry on the tradition of service, or "giving back." Several serve as attorneys representing tribal interests throughout the United States. John EchoHawk serves as the executive director of the Native American Rights Fund (NARF) in Boulder, Colorado.

This book grew from my strong desire to ensure that each of my grandchildren, and those who follow, learn of Echo Hawk and the proud heritage that belongs to them. I also felt that it was important to provide a place in this book for others to record the important stories of their names so that they will never forget their heritage.

Tremendous support has come from my entire family ever since the idea for this book was born the day I saw my granddaughter Savannah running in her beaded moccasins. I can see the influence of my family on the pages of this book, and I thank each family member for helpful ideas and insights. They have been as eager as I for this story to be preserved.